ON THE FARM

Alix Wood

WINDMILL BOOKS

Published in 2023 by Windmill Books,
an Imprint of Rosen Publishing
2544 Clinton St.
Buffalo, NY 14224

Copyright © 2023 Alix Wood Books

Produced for Rosen Publishing by Alix Wood Books
Designed by Alix Wood
Edited by Eloise Macgregor
Editor for Rosen: Kerri O'Donnell

Photo credits:
All images © Shutterstock; or in the public domain, with grateful thanks to the photographers who allowed them to be creative commons

All rights reserved. No part of this book may be reproduced in any form without permission in writing from the publisher, except by a reviewer.

Printed in the United States of America

CPSIA Compliance Information: Batch CWWM23
For Further Information contact Rosen Publishing at 1-800-237-9932

Cataloging-in-Publication Data

Names: Wood, Alix.
Title: On the Farm / Alix Wood.
Description: New York : Windmill Books, 2023. | Series: Odd one out | Includes answer key.
Identifiers: ISBN 9781538392553 (pbk) | ISBN 9781538392560 (library bound) | ISBN 9781538392577 (ebook)
Subjects: LCSH: Farm animals-- Juvenile literature
Classification: LCC SF75.5 W66 2023 | DDC 636/.01--dc23

Find us on

Can you find the odd one out? It's not always that easy!

The answers are on page 24

Which one is not ...

a sheep?

Can you spot who ...

is not a cow?

Which animal is not …

a goat?

Who is not a goose?

Which one is not ...

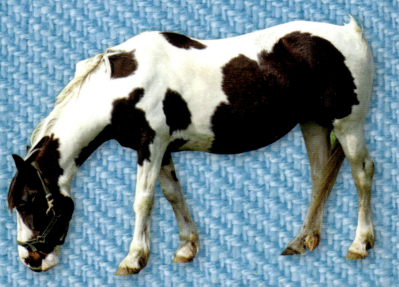

a horse?

Can you see who ...

is not a chicken?

One of these is ...

not a donkey.

Which animal isn't ...

a pig?

Find who isn't ...

an alpaca.

Who is not a duck?